ONE CAT'S SPECIAL CHRISTMAS

Lene Mayer-Skumanz
Ivan Gantschev

classic-minedition

On winter mornings Little Gray, the cat with the white spot
on the end of her tail, likes to stroll through the park. She walks
along secret paths that only cats know: from the yew tree to the
goose fountain, then looping back along the swans' lake to the
yew tree again. She enjoys lying underneath its thick, evergreen
branches. The ground feels nice here—warm and tingly, as if
a stream of sunbeams ran beneath it.

Her friends Old Tabby, Scarlet, Twilight, and Lumpy also like lounging under the yew tree. They prefer living outdoors in the park to staying indoors with people. They keep their distance when they see a human running through the park in the early morning hours, sweating and panting. The cats turn away, their tails twitching silently. Only Little Gray remembers a flash of something from her past, something special – a smell? A taste? A sound? She isn't sure what it might be. Images flicker through her mind like colorful shadows.

The sky is gray and cloudy. It smells of snow. Little Gray opens her eyes and peeks through the branches. She sees big white snowflakes everywhere! Suddenly her memory becomes clearer—she remembers a comforting blanket, a bowl of milk, a caressing hand, a faint and shaky voice. She remembers watching snowflakes whirling from behind a crystal-clear wall. And then one day it was all gone: the warmth, the bowl, the hand, the voice…

Little Gray crawls out from underneath the yew tree and sniffs at the air. Something feels different today.

People are raising a tall spruce tree next to the goose fountain. They fasten wires around its trunk. Other people erect wooden stalls. Little Gray hears banging and squeaking, and she ducks down in fear.

Little Gray waits for darkness to set in. She wants to go hunting, or rummage through the dumpsters. But tonight is neither dark nor silent. Lights blink, and lanterns swing from food carts. People smile and cheer. The wind carries different scents toward the yew tree—some are familiar, and some are new. The air is filled with ringing, humming, buzzing, and singing. Candles shine on top of a big wreath.

The park feels very different now. The sounds trickling from the lighted tree are tempting to investigate. But Little Gray's friend Twilight puts his ears back and hisses at the shoes and boots that walk too close. He lets out a meow that roughly translates to: "This is too much. Leave me alone."

Meanwhile, Lumpy just yawns. She knows that as long as the people are busy running about, they won't bother any cats hiding underneath the yew tree. She closes her eyes as if to say: "Forget these people." Little Gray twitches her tail in a motion that means: "No, I don't want to forget them." And she silently slinks away through the snow.

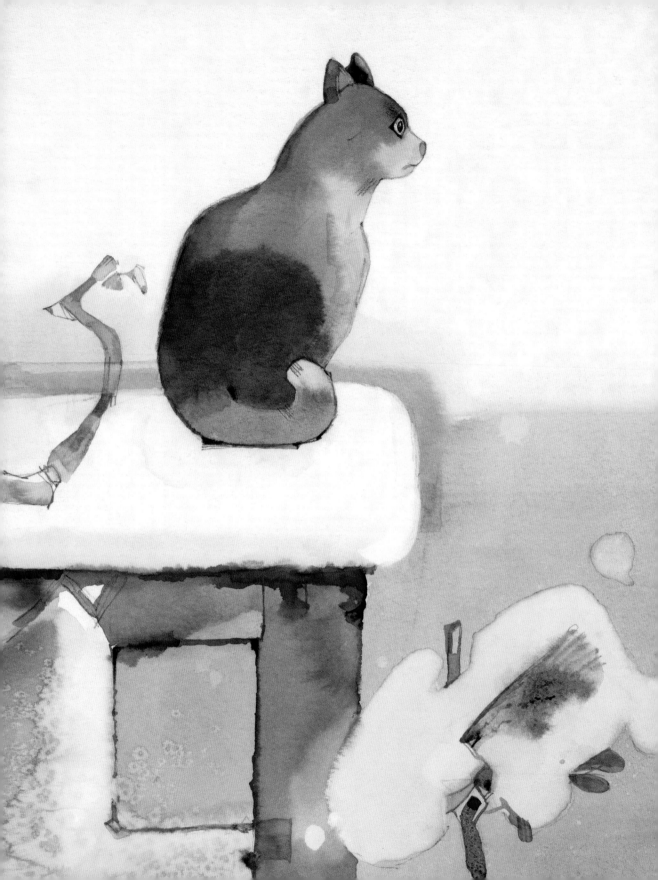

The statue near the swans' lake makes the perfect lookout spot for Little Gray. She watches all different kinds of people walk by who don't see her. She sits so still that not even the toddlers riding on their fathers' shoulders notice her. A windy shiver runs through Little Gray's fur. Her ears focus on a man who steps away from the teeming crowd. He walks up to the statue, the snow crunching underneath his feet. He moves very slowly.

Then the man looks up at Little Gray. "At last, a friendly face," he says. "This is what I was looking for." His voice is deep and jolly, and it sounds almost like a caress. "Now, smile, please," he says, holding a peculiar black box against his face. He turns and crouches, takes a step forward, then back. What a funny little dance!

The black box clicks and whirs. That makes Little Gray's fur stand up. Should she run away? But where to? "Look, little cat!" the man calls. "I have something to share with you." Little Gray hears a rustling sound and smells something delicious. Will the man share his food with her? Little Gray is suddenly very hungry.

The man walks on, searching for something. He
strolls around the lighted tree, looking for happy
faces in the Christmas market, for a gentle hand
perhaps, reaching out to a straw angel, or for
a shiny ornament which might reflect a smile.
He stops in front of the goose fountain again.
Little Gray sits on its edge. "Another one!"
says the man, laughing as he starts to do
his bend-and kneel dance again.

Little Gray sneaks back to the yew tree. She rubs her head against Old Tabby. "Don't leave us!" Old Tabby meows. Little Gray paces back and forth, one ear twisting to the right, one ear twisting to the left, listening. Her whiskers tremble. Her tail twitches. "I will be back!" she meows. "When the yew tree blossoms, I will return." And she leaps away through the branches.

Little Gray sniffs the air. Her human is still there, the man with the warm voice. He can't walk away now that she's chosen him, can he? The man spots a shadow dashing past. He sees Little Gray waiting at the corner. "Oh," he says with surprise. "Have we not met before?" "Meow," Little Gray answers.

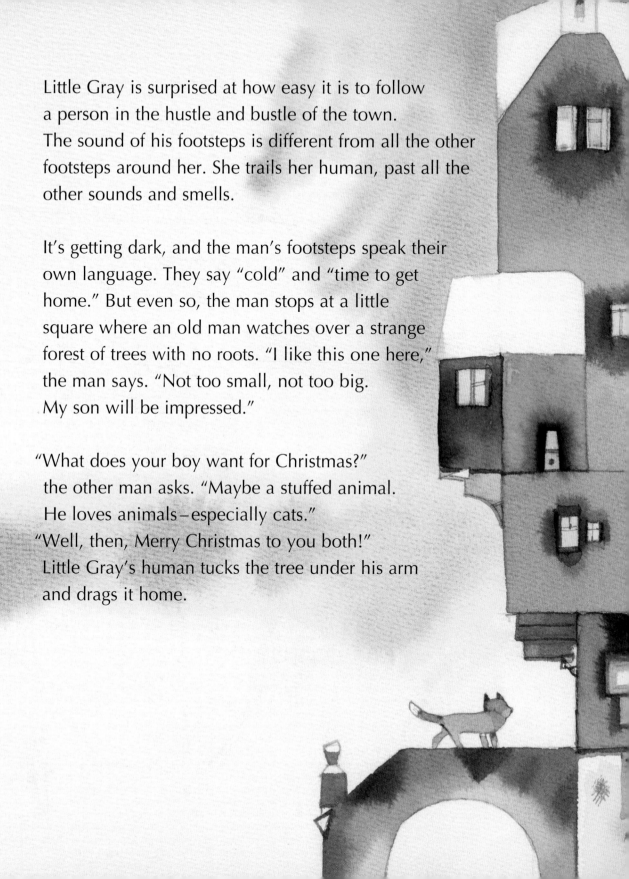

Little Gray is surprised at how easy it is to follow
a person in the hustle and bustle of the town.
The sound of his footsteps is different from all the other
footsteps around her. She trails her human, past all the
other sounds and smells.

It's getting dark, and the man's footsteps speak their
own language. They say "cold" and "time to get
home." But even so, the man stops at a little
square where an old man watches over a strange
forest of trees with no roots. "I like this one here,"
the man says. "Not too small, not too big.
My son will be impressed."

"What does your boy want for Christmas?"
the other man asks. "Maybe a stuffed animal.
He loves animals – especially cats."
"Well, then, Merry Christmas to you both!"
Little Gray's human tucks the tree under his arm
and drags it home.

The man carries the tree up some steep stairs. He leans
it against a white wall. He fumbles for his keys. "I'm here,
too!" Little Gray meows. "What! You?!" the man exclaims.
"Indeed, here you are!" Little Gray sits upright. She wraps
her tail with the white spot at the end around her front legs
and waits. "Well, I'm not sure…" the man says.

"Meow!" Little Gray insists. Then her human disappears behind
the front door. Little Gray lies down on the doormat. It smells
of different people, but it's not necessarily a bad smell.
She can hear footsteps from behind the door. Then it opens,
but only slightly. The man places a bowl of milk on the porch.
He whispers: "Be patient, we are still negotiating."

Little Gray drinks the milk with satisfaction. There's a feeling deep inside her, a feeling only cats know, telling her that she will be taken inside along with the tree. Maybe very soon.

You have to be patient with humans. They are not as quick and as certain as cats are.